WITCHES
of
BROOKLYN

Sophie Escabasse

WITCHES
of
BROOKLYN

Witches of Brooklyn was drawn with blue or purple pencils of all sorts, any brand will do, until they were two and a half inches long. Then all the sketches were scanned. Inking and coloring were done with Procreate and Photoshop.

Cover art, text, and interior illustrations copyright © 2020 by Sophie Escabasse
Case art used under license from Shutterstock.com

All rights reserved. Published in the United States by RH Graphic, an imprint of Random House Children's Books, a division of Penguin Random House LLC, New York.

RH Graphic with the book design is a registered trademark of Penguin Random House LLC.

Visit us on the Web! RHKidsGraphic.com • @RHKidsGraphic

Educators and librarians, for a variety of teaching tools, visit us at RHTeachersLibrarians.com

Library of Congress Cataloging-in-Publication Data is available upon request.
ISBN 978-0-593-11927-3 (pbk.) — ISBN 978-0-593-12528-1 (trade) — ISBN 978-0-593-11928-0 (lib. bdg.) — ISBN 978-0-593-11929-7 (ebook)

Designed by Patrick Crotty

MANUFACTURED IN CHINA
10 9 8 7 6 5 4
First Edition

A comic on every bookshelf.

For Patrick, my fabulous husband,
and our three amazing raccoons,
Ella, Josephine, and Arthur

Chapter 1

Let's get out of the car now. Come on. You have family waiting for you.

NOTHING is waiting for me here!

I'm not going!!

Oh YES you are!!

DO YOU KNOW WHAT TIME IT IS!!

¡¡¡iiiiiiiii!!!

Ahem, ahem.

I'm Agent "Joe" from adoption services.

I apologize for the late appearance. Are you Ms. Selimene Huchbolt-Walloo, sister of Emily Huchbolt-Walloo?

!?!! YES

This is your niece Effie. You are now her legal guardian. Ahem...your sister knew you would take good care of her daughter.

. . .

You should have been notified, but I have the documents if you want to see?

This is a joke, right?

Please be reasonable, that cannot be!

No mistake.

POOM

YOU HORRIBLE CARPET SELLER, YOU'RE GONNA LISTEN!! NO JELLYFISH WEARING SUNGLASSES AT NIGHT LIKE YOU ...

...IS GONNA FORCE ME TO DO ANYTHING!!

B-b-b... b-b...

Effie, isn't it? I'm Carlota. Let's go inside.

It's very late and you must be pretty tired. I know I am.

HOOLIGAN

Don't worry about Selimene. She'll calm down eventually.

GANGSTER!!! MISERABLE SPECIMEN OF HUMANITY!!

You can take Panda's room for now. He's barely ever here anymore, and I'm sure you'll like it. It's very bright during the day, and you'll have your privacy.

HERE WE ARE!

The bathroom is at the end of the corridor, my dear.

We'll show you the rest of the house tomorrow.

Sleep tight, my darling!

Don't worry, Woody. We won't stay here very long...

We don't need these weirdos...

There is **NO WAY** we're living with an eleven-year-old, Carlota! She can't stay here! How do you expect us to run the business with a kid underfoot?! It's madness!!

Kids go to school, Selimene.

And we've been talking about getting an apprentice for a while....

An apprentice for what?

SCUBA DIVING!

Good morning, my dear! How did you sleep?

Okay ...

Yes...that bed is rather comfortable.

I'll fix you a hot cocoa and show you around!

I hate hot cocoa! And I don't want to see your house. I'M NOT STAYING!!

You SiT!! And I know you love cocoa!

HEY!?

What...what just happened?

Hem...here's your cocoa, Effie, and you don't have to look at the house now if you don't feel like it.

!?!

Argh! They're having another of those gigantic music shows in the park. This time it's with someone called Tily Shoo.

Tily Shoo... what kind of name is that?

YOU DON'T KNOW WHO TILY SHOO IS? WHAT WORLD DO YOU LIVE IN?

She's THE biggest artist of the century!!

I have serious doubts about that, child.

11

She IS! You're just too old to see it.

She is NOT!! And you're too young to know anything about the century you live in!!

HMMPH

WOOF!

You have a cute dog. What's his name?

PURRR PURRR

Lion.

Lion? That's a funny name for such a small dog.

I guess you could say that he has his big moments.

Your name is lovely, by the way. Is it a family name?

Yes.

Or at least I think so.

Not like I have any REAL family around anymore to tell me.

What kind of names are Selimene and Carlota, anyway?

Respected and feared names with a loooong history!

And? Who cares? Sorry I asked.

Lovely child.

13

Would you like to look around now? We have some extraordinary books in the library.

I'M NOT READING!!

I'M NOT STAYING!!

Well...I'm afraid you may have to spend some time with us, my darling.

We understand it's very sudden...for us as well. And...of course, if for any reason...

OH! Don't give me that look, Lion!!

You win. I'm gonna go talk to her... She's a headache already!! And she's only been here for one night!

KNOCK!
KNOCK!

DON'T COME IN !!!

17

SIGH

I sometimes get carried away by emotions in the heat of the moment...I'm sorry that I hurt your feelings, Effie. I apologize.

You apologize...?!

Yes, I acted like a hideous old turtle, and I'm sorry.

I've never had a grown-up apologize to me...ever.

Mmh...

I did get a bit irritated with him... That's true...

Probably shouldn't have.

HA! A bit irritated! I wouldn't want to see what it's like when you're a lot irritated!

What do you think of this?

Honestly?

Here. You can put your beautiful T-shirts in here.

So...did you know anything about me...

...before last night?

I had no idea Emily felt that way...

Done!

Great!

C'mon! Let's show you around, cupcake!

WOW, easy on the nicknames, auntie! I'm no CUPCAKE!

Holy pineapple! It's gonna be fun to live with you!

Are those family pictures...?

Kind of. Family and friends.

You have an interesting-looking family.

Speaking of looks, I hope you don't mind me saying so, but you could use a good shower...and a comb.

I like your house...

And some fresh clothes...

It feels pretty gigantic... I've never lived in a place this big before.

And maybe an ear cleaning...?

Aah...okay, okay, can we see the rest of the house first?

Most certainly, my darling.

I brought some scones for the tour!

Mmm!

It's good!

You sensitive flower! I knew you had it in you!

Stop it!

Musical coconut! Cut it out!!

HE HE HE!!

GROUND FLOOR

PRIVATE DECK
FOR PRIVATE MATTERS

LIVING ROOM

SELIMENE
& CARLOTA'S
OFFICE

KITCHEN

GREENHOUSE

OUTDOOR TABLE
FOR SUMMER DINNER
AND GAMES

2ND FLOOR

Selimene's Bedroom

Bathroom

Carlota's Bedroom

Guest Bedroom

Cozy Sitting Room For Tea

3RD FLOOR

Bathroom

Effie's Bedroom

Closet

Yoga & Meditation Room

What do you do with all these plants?

These aren't regular plants, Effie. They have healing properties.

Never underestimate the power of nature, child! All these plants are used to heal people.

Wait a second. Does that mean you are doctors?

Sort of . . .

We are HERBALISTS, my dear.

. . . ?

You see, everyday aches and pains don't require heavy chemicals. For centuries, people have used plants to heal them!

And how do you turn a plant into a medicine, exactly? Do you have a lab or something?

Should we show you the rest of the house, my dear?

YES! Let's keep moving or we'll be here all day!

!?

I hate when people avoid my questions.

What are they hiding?

And here is the acupuncture office.

Ew! You stick needles into people?

OH MY, oh my. I need to sit!

You, child, definitely have a sense of drama.

The needles we use are very light and thin, Effie. Nothing like sewing needles.

Yes, but, but...

THEY'RE NEEDLES!

Special needles. You don't even feel them.

And acupuncture is back in fashion, my darling!

It's true that it's making a comeback!

With good reason! It makes you feel better!

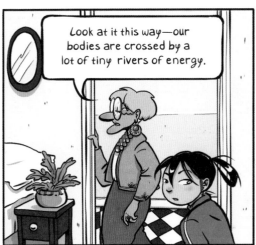

Look at it this way—our bodies are crossed by a lot of tiny rivers of energy.

If the flow gets blocked, needles help reopen the path.

And what's behind this door?

Just a messy unfinished basement. Nothing you want to see...

HMMPH. Okay.

Let's get a couple more of Carlota's delicious scones before throwing you in the shower.

So...people come here for appointments and stuff?

Right.

In fact, I'm expecting someone in ten minutes.

ARGH... I almost forgot it's Thursday.

Oh! So it's decided?

I'm so happy, Effie!!

Welcome aboard, Cupcake!

Driiiing! Driing!!

Ah, if you'll excuse me, ladies.

CARLOTA!! I'VE BEEN DYING ALL WEEK!! MY PINKY IS KILLING ME!

See?

But tell me, my dear. What about registering you for school today?

What is she doing?! We're going to be late!

We're only two minutes away from the school, Selimene. We're good.

I'm ready.

And that's what took you so long?! Jeans and a sweater?

YES! And I love it! Thank you!

You look lovely! Now let's go or we'll be late.

You're going to be fine, Effie. It's normal to be anxious on your first day.

I remember...I always loved having new kids in my class.

The fun of discovering someone new...

Seeing if the book's cover matches the inside...

?

Right. And if some kids aren't nice, just punch them in the nose!

HA HA HA HA!

SELIMENE!! HOW CAN YOU SAY THINGS LIKE THAT?!

I'm only joking, Carlota.

I wanted to see if I could get her to smile.

Here we are, Effie. Do you remember where you have to go?

Yes...we've toured the school a million times! I could draw a map by heart.

She'll be fine, Selimene.

Of course she will!

EFFIE!

Class! I want to introduce you to our new student, Effie.

Effie just arrived in town, and I'm counting on you to show her how welcoming we are in Brooklyn.

You'll sit next to Oliver and Berrit, Effie.

Okay.

Hi!

Hi!

For the next hour, we'll be working on our group projects. Berrit, Oliver, please include Effie in your group.

Our project is on the Sumerians, who were amazingly inventive people.

So the cuneiform writing was...

Maybe you can let go of her now, Berrit...

It's okay.

YES! SORRY, OF COURSE!

...and the Mesopotamians.

Astrid. Always showing off! I can't believe she brought a phone to school!!

It's sooo forbidden!

OH MY GOD!! IS IT THE "X12"?!

SHHH... OF COURSE IT IS!!

Do you have a smartphone, Effie?

Me?! I bet my aunt doesn't even know what it is!

Both my brother and sister have one.

And did delirious joy overflow in their lives when they got it...?

Haha!! No, but they were happy enough!

I just think you're investing too much in owning a smartphone, that's all.

It's great to have one, sure, but think about all the time you waste with it! You miss so much of real life.

So did you have to punch anyone today?

HA! HA! HA!

I've met two very cool kids. I'm sitting next to them in class.

And guess what? One is an orphan too!

You talked about that already?

OH! And do you two know what a smartphone is?

We may be old, but we don't live in a cave, you know!

Believe it or not, we have INTERNET in this house!

NO WAY!

YES WAY!

Now, if you'll excuse me, I have a patient in two minutes.

MOM...

STOP!!! I'M AWAKE.

COULD YOU STOP SENDING LION TO WAKE ME UP?! It's a very stressful start to the day, you know?!

But he loves it so much! And I feel like his voice has improved a lot! Don't you?

Grrr...

Is Archibald picking you up today?

ARCHI-WHO?!...WHAT?!

ARCHIBALD. Oliver's au pair. We're going to walk to school together.

DRIIING - DRIING DRIING-

IT'S THEM!

They live a couple of blocks away, they're in the same class...it's perfect, Selimene.

ORNING

YEEES...

ARGH... SELIMENE!S

AAH... CAN WE GO NOW?

HAVE A GREAT DAY, CHILDREN!

SEE YOU LATER.

Goodbye, Ms. Huchbolt-Walloo!

Not sure about his babysitting skills, but I love the style of that Archi-Ball...

ARCHIBALD, Selimene. His name is Archibald.

Is your grandmother in fashion, Effie?

WHAT!! NO WAY! She's an acupuncturist.

Ah, okay...she seems very special...

Tell me about it!

AT RECESS

Would you both like to come over to my place this weekend?

GUESS where my dad is taking me this weekend?!

TILY SHOO'S concert in Central Park!

WOW!

What a SHOW-OFF!

?

Who cares about Tily Shoo, anyway?

WE DO!

GEEZ! SORRY!

Anyway, I'd be happy to come over this weekend...Thanks for the invitation.

Of course we'll come over!!

That night around 1 a.m.

RING-DRIING-DRING-DRIING-DRI

mm?

NOT AGAIN!!!

Good evening. I mean, good morning. Sorry for intruding.

(. . .)

Is it me or has our house just been taken over?!

BY A BUNCH of HOOLIGANS!

I'LL BLOW YOU TO BITS!! CRIMINALS!

GET OUT OF MY HOUSE!!

THIS is PRIVATE PROPERTY! YOU BRUTES!!

I hope your story is good, because I'm about to call the cops on you!

Geez! Carlota...

DON'T! LISTEN. WE HAVE A SITUATION HERE.

A pretty peculiar situation, which requires special care, or should I say a miracle?

Sigh.

Okay. You have our attention, lady. Exactly what happened to your pop star?

Well... Tily?

BOOOOO

Could you please stop sobbing for a minute and tell your story?

Yes.

Snif! Snif!

It all started at that terrible party at my friend Henry's.

And the next morning, I woke up like this!! I called Diane right away.

And we've tried absolutely everything since then.

TUUT TUUU TUUT TUUT

Well, you're pretty naive...

Shhh...Selimene! What exactly do you mean by "everything"?

Skin creams, lasers, all kinds of face washes, clays, scrubs...we even tried placing leeches on my chin to see if it would affect the color!

?!

But more seriously... Why don't you give it some time? It may go away by itself.

BUT WE DON'T HAVE TIME!!

I have to be onstage this weekend! In two days!

In two days!

Two days...

Hmm...

Could I get...

...some coffeeeee...too...

There are a couple of things I can think of that we could try relatively easily.

I'LL DO ANYTHING!!

I NEED A MIRACLE!

Money

isn't

a problem.

Oh, it's really not about money, my dear.

If money could buy peace of mind and a heart filled with joy, we wouldn't be here, right?

We'll start by doing our best and see where that takes us, but you can really thank our...

WOOF

...niece.

Are you guys having a party?

Not quite.

TILY SHOO

Here is someone who recognizes you.

I AM SUCH A FAN!!! YOUR LAST ALBUM IS KILLER!! THE SONG "MAYBE YOU'LL REMEMBER ME NOW," OH MY GOSH, IT BLOWS MY MIND!!! AND Y... ...YOUR... VOICE OF...

COUGH COUGH

Very nice. Thank you, child. Now if you wouldn't mind going back to wherever you came from, we have very serious issues to discuss here, and a young superfan is the last thing we need!

Am I coming down with something?

Dizzy...

Oh no! I think I'm gonna be sick!

?!

EXCUSE ME!

?!

In front of Tily Shoo! That's so embarrassing!

CLICK

What's wrong with me?!

We're gonna put you in the living room. It will be...

I need socks and gloves!!

Where are you?

You're really something special, Lion. Thank you.

Make yourselves comfortable. It may take a little while.

OOOH! MY LITTLE PUMPKIN!!

CARLOTA!! CARLOTA, COME SEE!!

GASP!

I knew it...I'm dying! The day I meet my idol, I'm dying!!

You're not dying, you silly goose!! You're a witch!!

How long do I have?!

89

Chapter 3

click!

Are you coming, pumpkin?

I THINK SHE'S TAKING ROOT.

AARH!!

WHAT IS THAT?!

Calm down with the fluorescent business, pumpkin. You'll be fine!

The glow in your nails is only temporary. In a week you won't see it anymore.

So I'm only a witch for a week?!

Ha ha ha! No, my dear. A witch is a witch for life!

And...what does a witch do, exactly?

That's the beauty of it. Anything!

You can do anything you want. Being a witch doesn't mean you have to act like a cartoon villain!

Selimene and I decided to use our powers to help others. To make it easier and not scare anyone, we present ourselves as acupuncturists and herbalists. Which we are, but not only.

Why would they be scared if you want to help?

Because the unknown is scary, my pumpkin. People are afraid of what they cannot name or understand.

Does that mean we have to hide our powers?

It's more like masking them. But yes.

Why did my powers decide to appear now?

I'm not joking. You will have to train!

YOUNG PADAWAN!

HA HA HA HA!

Hilarious, Francis!

Training IS important. But we should really start looking at our red singer problem, my darlings.

Tily Shoo! I almost forgot!

She wasn't looking like her usual self.

But even in red, she's super pretty.

Don't you think?

100

A super gigantic ego is what I saw!

Hmmm.

She's a star!

Well, for now, she's red. What did you have in mind, Carlota?

I think we should start with a strong curse removal.

What are those, Selimene?

Straws.

From a special kind of hay. Here, you may find this amusing...

Walk slowly over here, Effie. Pretend you're carrying a cup of hot tea that you don't want to spill.

I don't drink tea.

Perfect.

What is that thing, Carlota? It looks like it's alive. Is it?

It is sort of alive. It's pollen, my dear. Nothing like Nephlar's pollen to break a curse!

And what's that?!

Humbint. It's rather unusual to put it in a curse removal potion.

But we've had great success with it. Just changed the composition slightly.

And what is this, Selimene?

GOOD LORD! YOU NEVER STOP ASKING QUESTIONS, DO YOU?!

How do you expect her to learn if she doesn't ask questions?

Asking questions is wonderful, Francis!

SO SORRY! I HADN'T REALIZED WE'D ALL LOST OUR SENSE OF HUMOR!

So this is another kind of rarity that we grow down here, my dear. It's a fungus.

Here! We're almost ready to go!

Now your mental state becomes important. You have to be calm, confident, and positive.

Try to visualize the waves washing over the sand.

It never gets old.

Are you coming, pumpkin? Time to see what your singer looks like without the red!

I'll call you back.

READY?

Would you mind coming to our office, Tily?

YES!

I mean NO! I'm coming. MARTIN! You're coming too!

We'll wash your face with the potion first.

Then you will drink two tablespoons of it.

Don't worry. You'll be fine.

Do you feel anything?

Let me make sure I've got this straight. You've tried a...a wide spectrum antidote, but it didn't work. Obviously. And now...?

Now we'll try a more targeted approach.

Right. And how long will that take, exactly?

We'll do our best, and that's all I can tell you for now!

C'mon, child. Let's put you to bed.

I don't want to go to bed! I want to help you!

That's very noble.

You can barely keep your eyes open, my darling. There will be plenty to help with tomorrow. Off you go!

DRILLING

That's Oliver and Archibald!

WAIT!

Not exactly your style, I know.

?

But you keep it! It's an order.

If anything happens, rub it twice on your nose.

Got it?

I rub the old thing on my nose twice.

Oookay...

See you!

Take care, kid.

Fingers crossed.

Fingers crossed.

115

Morning!

WAIT!

?!?

?

WAIT!
Wait! Your lunch!!

Who was that?

A friend of my aunt's...

He's a...chef. Loves to cook.

He couldn't even touch his breakfast this morning.

UGH.

How is your stress level? Feeling ready?

I know I'm being ridiculous. I shouldn't be stressed...I just can't help it.

Good morning, class. We'll start the day with the group presentations. Berrit, Effie, Oliver!

You go first.

I expect everyone to be attentive and respectful.

HA!

HAHA

Democracy means "ruled by the people," from the Greek: demos— "people"— and kratos—"rule." It's a political system that appeared in the fifth century in some cities in Greece, like Athens. In the early days of democracy, women and people of color were not included. Not fair! It would be some time before everyone had rights.

In a democracy, we the people have the power! We organize elections where each citizen gets to vote on our leaders. It's a big responsibility. We're the ones who decide! Yay!! It's much more fair than a monarchy, where only a king or an emperor decides everything and doesn't have to answer to anyone about anything he does. The US system of government is a republic. That means we elect people who will then run the government, like the president, the members of Congress, and...

(. . .)

(. . .)

(. . .)

? . . . . . . ?

DEMOCRACY!

HA-HA HA HA HA HA HA HA HO HA HA Hi-H

Can we please remain calm until the end of our classmates' presentation?

Democracy is important because it's the form of government that provides its citizens with the most freedom and ensures that fundamental human rights are granted to each citizen.

DEMO CRACY!

DEMOCRACY.

At least it's over with.

DEMO

The painting is empty!

SHUT

?

We...we're safe now. The snake can't go anywhere.

It was a huge python, Principal Jones, HUGE!

Hello, fire department?!

I want you to find books you like and read in small groups. I'll be back!

SHHH...

Did I do that...?

Only one way to be sure.

Come to life. Come to life. Come to life.

BUTERFL

No...I'll be fine. I'm halfway through the day. How is Tily Shoo? Did you guys make any progress?

We're working on something. But it takes time, so you'll be home before we're done with it.

Great! I have to go now, but... about the snake? What if the firefighters take him away? The painting will be empty!

Don't worry about it. When you left the room, your magic dissipated. The snake will have returned to his frame.

Where were you?! I was worried about you.

Here she is.

Sorry, guys...I had a bad stomachache.

It must be that snake. Such a wild story!! A python!!!

Er...thank you... Right. The snake.

It's pretty far from home.

Let's go eat! All these emotions made me starving!

WHOA!! Fancy sandwich!!

You know, if you're feeling sick, we don't have to come over this weekend.

Yeah, you don't look so good. We can always come by later.

Ha! No, I'll be fine. You have to come.

Well, if you insist.

What if we call each other on Saturday morning?

Perfect.

You take it easy today and see how you feel tomorrow.

Works for me!

What are the chances the firefighters got the snake, you think?

I'm sure they got it! We'll know in a minute. It's time to go meet Ms. Pratt in the lobby.

SIGH

Listen up, class! The firefighters couldn't find the snake, so we'll go back to the library.

But we're clear to go get our belongings. We'll do so calmly, two at a time, and we'll meet in the library. Understood?

Please, please, let the snake be back in the painting.

Phew!

Hurry up, Effie!

Please, please.

Whoa...what are you doing, Selimene?

I'm writing Doris Mc Finn's story down, my pumpkin. This parchment paper and the ink I'm using are both enchanted.

It will capture and bring to life the story that I write.

NEAT!

Neat but powerful! One has to be very careful when using journey parchment!

Ick!!

You should use it sparingly and change only tiny details of your story, because it will change your life.

That's pretty bad, Selimene! Can you change it?

Too late.

Hello, everyone!

Are we going into your office again?

You will be comfier over here. But if your crew could go wait in the kitchen, it would help.

I need at least one assistant!

I guess Martin can stay.

Of course "emotional support Martin" can stay.

We'll put her in the center of the room.

That should make enough room, Martin. Thank you.

I've read that you've been singing and writing songs since you were a little girl.

It must be SO amazing to create music...Do you dream of music sometimes?

Mmm...

BURP

?

?

OH NO!

Aie!

SiGH

SiGH

SiGH

So I guess that didn't work either.

!

BLARGY

Red-face! Would you please calm down?

They're only trying to help you, Tily.

SHUSH, MARTIN!

I DON'T NEED YOUR RIDICULOUS PEP TALK!! YOU'RE A LOSER!

A RIDICULOUS LOSER !!

Stomp! Stomp!

Nothing like a diva's tantrum after a sleepless night.

CUT IT OUT!

What...?

YOU CAN'T TALK TO PEOPLE LIKE THIS!! YOU'RE SO RUDE AND NASTY!!

Chapter 4

What I don't get is that the things we tried last night and this afternoon should have cured any curse you could encounter!

We must have forgotten something. Think, Carlota, Think!

My brain has turned into cauliflower. It's hopeless.

I KNOW, RIGHT?! I'M SO GOOD-NATURED!

YOUNG ONE? YOU, WHO'S STILL FLEXIBLE.

WOULD YOU MIND PLACING THAT BOOK ON THE TOP SHELF, RIGHT-HAND SIDE, NEXT TO THE BLUE ONE, PLEASE?

Sure,

I THINK I'VE GOT SOMETHING!

"...And that would clear their faces and allow them to be called Vermilion witches."

Could some of their sacred cream have lasted all these years?

Some things last for centuries, Carlota. Look at Francis's bad temper.

I HEARD YOU!

That or we're facing a group of "modern" Vermilion witches... That's interesting.

It is true that clear magic is a thing we haven't tried yet... We've tried potions and rituals, and Tily's people have tried science and technology, but...

Sorry to interrupt, Carlota.

What is clear magic, exactly?

It's natural magic, pumpkin. The oldest form of magic known. It uses the power of the elements. Pretty basic.

YOU'RE RIGHT, CARLOTA!

She's her true best self when she's playing her music. We just have to make her sing again!

Why not...it's worth trying. But will that be enough to make the red go away...?

The book doesn't give any details on the final ceremony.

Don't forget the other aspect of what she does, Selimene. She sings FOR people.

It will be the best day of Berrit's life!!

Mmh...

Let's call first to see if your friends can come, power bean. It's already almost five in the evening.

"Power bean"? Really...?

You go, and I'll keep looking for the details about the ceremony.

I suggest that you say you're inviting them for a movie night.

Good idea. I wouldn't know how to explain the situation on the phone anyway.

Hello, Oliver? Hi! It's Effie. Would you like to come over to watch a movie tonight? Yes, sure! Archibald too. Okay. See ya!

Oliver and Archibald are in!

Good!

You know what, Selimene?

I've never used a phone like this! It's like in the old movies!

SIGH

Hello, Mrs. Rossi? Good evening, it's Effie.

Could Berrit come over tonight to watch a movie with Oliver and me?

Of course I'll put her on.

She wants to talk to you.

Hello?

Yes...I understand. No, no, it's not a problem at all. My pleasure. Eight-thirty, right. A lovely evening to you too!

SO?

We're good! We'll have to drive her home afterward.

I love the idea of dumping rain on our despotic musical sea lion!

Wait! You can make rain?

Selimene is extremely gifted with meteorological events, my darling. Clouds, wind, and electricity, obviously.

I'll show you, pumpkin. It's not that hard. But you seem to have the ability to bring two-dimensional things to life!

We should definitely explore that. I was impressed with your wallpaper effect earlier!

Thank you...

But I really don't know how I do it...

Which is a bit scary.

And I wonder if I could do it when I was a baby too. Is that possible?

We believe we've found the key to your...hum...to our problem.

WHAT are you talking about?

The fact that we couldn't alter the time—

—tells us we're facing very strong magic.

And our first attempts at curse removal didn't work either because—

—the spell you're under is beyond us.

SO THERE'S NO CURE? YOU CAN'T HELP ME?!

Sit down, sea lion. Carlota isn't done!

Sea what?

Ahem...in light of this discovery, we believe YOU must be the one to free yourself.

But...but how?

You see, the Vermilion witches would apply this cream at the beginning of their training—

—and the color was an indicator of success. Only when they had found their own path would the red color go away.

Obviously you're not a witch in training who has vowed to serve others.

But we strongly believe that your gift for singing is the key.

You haven't performed since the incident, have you?

OF COURSE NOT!

We think that you should.

WHAT!?

Only in front of a very small audience.

OUT OF THE QUESTION!

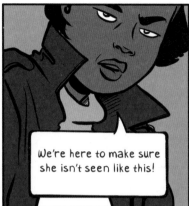

We're here to make sure she isn't seen like this!

It will only be us and three of Effie's friends.

The idea is to re-create the pattern of the Vermilion witches. We need you to do what you do best, and do it for others.

NO!

Not your face or your hair or your clothes.

Last night when I met you in the kitchen, I didn't even notice your face was red!

I was just so happy to meet you!

?

WEII DONE!

You saved the day, pumpkin! That was brilliant!

Thank you...

I'm sure it wasn't easy for you to say all these nice things to Tily. You rock, girl. Thank you.

What can I say?
I have a heroic soul!

A "heroic soul"...
Right.

I'll remember that the next time we need you to take the trash out!

HA HA HA.

Sorry to interrupt.
Tily is settled. Could I use your printer now?

Of course! We have a heroic soul here, eager to help you.

In the office, I presume?

Yes.

I'll get you back, Selimene.

HA! HA! HA!

I'll go make some tapas for our visitors.

?

Why on earth are you bothering being a pop star's assistant when you're SO obviously in love with cooking and feeding people, my friend?

Chapter 5

202

You have no idea how much of a treat...

?

?

This way!

Guys, this is Martin. Martin, meet my friends Berrit, Oliver, and Archibald.

Welcome, everyone!

!

!

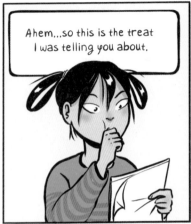

Ahem...so this is the treat I was telling you about.

Papers don't look like a treat to me.

They're not the treat. The treat is that... well, we're not watching a movie.

Then what are we doing?

We're having a private concert.

But we won't be able to talk about it. That's why we have to sign these papers.

WHAT!

ARE YOU SERIOUS ?!

Yes.

I'm gonna meet Tily Shoo...I can't believe it. This is the BEST DAY of my life!

Tell me, Effie...How exactly do you get a world-renowned singer to sing for you AND your friends...

...here at your house?

It's a dream, Oliver. We're living a dream.

You know... my aunts have so many connections!

"So many connections," right...

So many connections ...

Oh my garnish!
Is that child
all right?

I'm fine!! It's the best
day of my life! Thank you
so much!!

You see?
I told you!

Let's go sit in the front!

She should be here in a minute.

CLICK TAP

Did it...?

¡IT WORKED!

Well, she got me. Who knew so much power and beauty was hidden beneath that facade.

There's the artist and there's the art. Very artistic rain, by the way. Well done!

MARTIN! TOWELS, QUICK!

ROBERT! KEVIN! START PACKING UP!

Excuse me...
Could...could I have
your autograph?

Please?

Sure! What's
your name?

Berrit.

Ahem.

?

Could I have one
too, please?

You?

Me.

Let's go back inside
before we freeze!

I can't believe what we just saw... I had to ask for an autograph to make it real.

What are you talking about?

To prove to myself when I wake up tomorrow morning that I didn't just dream it!

Right...

I totally get it.

Thank you.

THANK YOU!

I feel silly now.

Don't.

You see?! I told you!

Well, you have to admit that the song that was everywhere last summer is pretty average!

Blah blah.

It's impossible to have a conversation with you!

Oh, come on!

Oliver...

We should probably be going. It's getting late.

Hey, Martin!
Are you planning
on helping?

Not anymore, Robert!

I QUIT.

We may have room for another VIP...

I mean...not to the city, but to my place. It's on your way!! I've always dreamed of riding in a limousine!

Fine with me. Martin, you're in charge of making sure Berrit gets into her building!

No problem, Captain!

YAY! BYE, GUYS!

Well done!

Acknowledgments

Thank you to Kelly Sonnack, my extraordinary, amazing agent, for her support, guidance, and wisdom. This book wouldn't exist if our paths hadn't crossed. Thank you for believing in me—I am so grateful to you for being my agent.

Thanks to the Random House team, especially to Gina Gagliano for being such an amazing human being and believing in me and the Witches of Brooklyn from the beginning.

Thank you to Whitney Leopard for her incredible work editing this book. Thank you for your patience and kindness with all my questions and typos.

I am also very grateful to Patrick Crotty for his help shaping this book and bringing it to life. And for recommending so many cool graphic novels to me.

Thank you to my husband, Patrick Flynn, for loving and supporting me and being by my side through all the ups and downs of the birth of this book. (Another birth!)

Thanks to my incredible children, Ella, Josephine, and Arthur, for being the best and for being so enthusiastic about everything I draw.

Thank you to my amazing, loving parents for being my first cheerleaders and for introducing me to the work of André Franquin (a Belgian comic artist who made me fall in love, once and for all, with comics).

And finally, thanks to Crouton for her unwavering love and support.

Sophie Escabasse is a French illustrator and comic artist living in Brooklyn, New York, with her husband and three children. She has illustrated books for middle-grade readers, including Kenzie Kickstarts a Team (The Derby Daredevils #1) by Kit Rosewater and the Spotlight Club Mysteries series by Florence Parry Heide and Roxanne Heide Pierce.

Sophie studied graphic design at the École nationale supérieure des Arts Décoratifs in Paris and at Central Saint Martins College of Art and Design. She worked in advertising in Paris and New York for a couple of years before fully embracing illustration as a career.

Hailing from a family of graphic novel lovers, Sophie has been enjoying comics since she learned to read. Today she's happily juggling being a mom of three and a comic artist of a new trilogy. It's a lot of sweat but a lot of fun!

Witches of Brooklyn is her graphic novel debut.

THERE GOES THE NEIGHBORHOOD!

EFFIE (AND HER MAGICAL AUNTS!) RETURNS IN A BRAND-NEW SEQUEL

RH
GRAPHIC

Sophie Escabasse

Witches
of
Brooklyn

MAGIC, FANTASY, AND WONDER— ALL IN A GRAPHIC NOVEL

Aster and the Accidental Magic
by Thom Pico and Karensac

After a trickster spirit gives Aster three wishes, her new home suddenly gets interesting!

Kerry and the Knight of the Forest
by Andi Watson

There's a deep, dark forest on Kerry's way home. Will he find his way through or be trapped there forever?

Séance Tea Party
by Reimena Yee

Lora doesn't want to grow up—can her new ghost-friend, Alexa, change her mind?

Doodleville
by Chad Sell

Drew's art is getting out of control . . . and escaping off the page!

Witches of Brooklyn
by Sophie Escabasse

Life in Brooklyn takes a strange turn when Effie discovers MAGIC runs in the family. . . .

5 Worlds
by Mark Siegel, Alexis Siegel, Xanthe Bouma, Matt Rockefeller, and Boya Sun

The Five Worlds are in danger. Can three unlikely heroes come together to save everyone?

VISIT US AT RHKIDSGRAPHIC.COM